FRICTION

BOOKS BY MATT MARSHALL

The Starlight Line
Friction

FRICTION

MATT MARSHALL

CAGED LETTER PRESS

Chapters VII, XI, XII, XV, XVIII, XXII, XXVII and XXXIV appeared previously in the *Guide to Kulchur Creative Journal*, no. 6.

Article referenced and quoted on pages 7–8: Terry Pluto, "Easter Brings Forgiveness and Lifting of Guilt's Weight," *The Plain Dealer*, April 19, 2014.

Special thanks to Andrew Fedynsky, director emeritus and resident scholar of the Ukrainian Museum-Archives, for his assistance with research into the blasphemy case against Taras Shevchenko.

I

If April is indeed the cruellest month as Eliot assured us all those years ago then the height of its cruelty might well have been its giving me to light as Spanish speakers would have it on a steely cruel day some 30 odd years back the icy winds whipping through my mother's sweat-drenched hair tangling with her screams as I was made to understand and thus keeping her there confined to the hospital bed for an additional few weeks owing to her newly caught pneumonia why the windows were left open in

the hospital room to begin with I haven't a clue
nor was I given even the breath of an explanation
though perhaps I was never born in such a clinical
spot but out in a field or some such unlikely place
but no matter I am here and that is enough to testify
to April's cruel nature I think you will agree but
then I am getting ahead of myself or behind myself
maybe the simple fact of the matter which of course is
anything but simple is that Angelika is now dead done
in by her own hand again typically in April a year ago
as April is the month when the number of suicides
jumps suddenly to ride out the summer on its
plateau of death so I guess we can say that in this
one instance and perhaps in this instance alone
Angelika was the leader of the pack which she no
doubt would have found rather terrifying enough
so in fact that if someone had pointed out the
leadership quality of her suicide it might well have
been enough to stay her hand on that fateful day and
keep her here with us but that train I'm afraid has
left the station attesting again to April's blind

delirious cruelty although of course one shouldn't imply that the fourth month or any month for that matter is some kind of conscious agent looking to do us harm but instead only happens to fall owing to no fault of its own in a season at least in the northern hemisphere that seems to compel us toward violence maybe leading one to opine that April is but a label we give to a particularly strong mode of human aggression

I first met Angelika as she was coming off the velodrome on Broadway not to insinuate that there's some other velodrome in town and maybe not another in the state even she was walking her bike which I recall as making a rather disturbing clicking noise or at least one that was disturbing to me but what do I know about bikes? and she was grinning broadly completely oblivious to the noise apparently so for all I know that clicking was in fact an indication of the machine's good health which indeed may have accounted for her smile although I chose yes I think it's fair to say that I chose to believe that she was instead smiling at me although we had

never met and had never knowingly laid eyes upon
one another but her smile had such a congenial
effect as to trigger within me the warm
remembrance of some past love or other whom I
couldn't to be honest put my finger on so it wouldn't
be right to say that she reminded me of a particular
former girlfriend or of any other woman I had known
but simply felt supremely familiar and
supremely friendly as she approached me and
smiled even more broadly as it seems to me now so
that I wished her a good morning which she
reciprocated with such a sudden blush of joy
that it made me feel she'd been waiting weeks for a
chance to respond to such a greeting having
apparently kept her silence until just such a moment
compressing her anticipation all the while later we went to
breakfast or perhaps it would be better to call it
brunch maybe it was lunch already she ordered an
omelet in any event and I believe I ordered some
kind of sandwich and after our coffee and her juice
arrived she began to talk about Donetsk and her

mixed feelings about the uproar there with the pro-Russian militants taking over various government buildings and demanding greater autonomy within Ukraine her paternal grandfather being from Donetsk she had spent a few summers there as a child and had very fond romantic memories of the place processed in faded green with the scent of ripening apples and the comforting murmur of Russian I stupidly asked what the political mood had been there at the time whether some people were even then yearning to be embraced again by Russia but of course she hadn't had the least idea about such things as a child a fact she confirmed with a sudden boisterous laugh which to my ear seemed more forceful than necessary although there was nothing cruel in it and was actually so altogether inviting that I was just as suddenly laughing with her she recalled her grandfather's house as a large unadorned rectangular structure of two stories that shimmered a ghostly white at nightfall and often featured candles in the windows that cast an intense light onto the lane that ran closely by the front door but truly she couldn't be sure if that had been her grandfather's house or rather the painting of some country house that she had seen somewhere perhaps one by Magritte though she had fixed the house there in her mind for so long that it was now firmly and probably irrevocably set amidst the nighttime noises of frogs and crickets and the brush of a crisp cotton nightgown against her skin and after all that house might just as well have belonged to her grandfather as any other

It occurred to her recently that her grandfather might actually have been a heroin addict a notion brought on by her own therapy sessions for the affliction it's an epidemic you know she said that morning during breakfast or lunch even as deaths from prescription opiate overdose are falling the number from heroin is on the rise it's really just a matter of cost it's a whole lot cheaper you know she went quiet then for a while and slowly and rather sadly it seemed to me chewed her omelet which had arrived during our discussion of her grandfather's house and the summers she had spent in Donetsk which must have been longer and more involved than I remember the discussion that is not the time she spent in Donetsk to account sufficiently for the time required to prepare our breakfast or her breakfast rather and my lunch I asked her how long she had used heroin which seemed a wholly natural appropriate and unintrusive question at the time but strikes me now as quite forward shockingly so in fact but she was not at all put off by the question and even seemed to welcome it as I recall looking up from her plate with her fork just inserted into the omelet to tell me that it had been about this same time of year so one might say that she was commemorating an anniversary of sorts albeit one she'd have preferred not to have been a part of but there it was she first shot up on a Good Friday six years prior and it quickly became her cross to bear she grinned which caused me to mention a silly article I had read in the paper that morning which posited Christ's crucifixion as the conclusion and quite a reasonable one in the author's view of an established atonement tradition that sacrificed animals and crops to cover the sins of humans and that Christ's blood had represented the ultimate sacrifice "so that people no longer had to kill things to be forgiven" which suggests that killing plants and animals was in fact a valid God-endorsed manner of absolving human foibles and misdeeds before this a completely ridiculous notion of course but then aren't most notions of faith I used to think my death would be a type of sacrifice she said flatly returning to her omelet and we didn't talk again about her heroin use until several weeks later a fact I attribute now to my untimely and inconsiderate mention of the stupid newspaper article

After we had finished eating and paid the bill we went out and chatted a bit longer on the sidewalk finally I asked how far of a ride she had back to her place to which she replied with a laugh while unlocking her bike not far and why the laugh? nothing it's only that it's a track bike it has no brakes yes? so I'll get there fast no matter the distance ah yes I see ha she shrugged maybe disappointed I hadn't laughed all that freely but I mean really and by this time it must have already been early afternoon I have the feeling that I was late for something or other but I can't for the life of me recall what it might have been or if it even was most likely it was nothing of any great importance as I'm often plagued by anxiety over remaining in one place for too long a time always I'm anxious to move on and when the need strikes me it wants to be satisfied immediately to get on to that other place and hurry and on that afternoon I think my discomfort must have been obvious to Angelika for it seems to me that seconds after my shrug she was already halfway down the block walking her bike and as she turned the corner I realized that I had failed to acquire any contact information hadn't even learned her last name in fact so I stood there dumb for quite a while kicking myself but finally wow I remember it as several minutes standing there but of course it couldn't have been that long when I finally turned from the sidewalk

that no longer held Angelika and got in my car and
drove home or to that other important unimportant place
that I so desperately needed to be

II

In those days I was maintaining myself as
something of an academic specializing in an area of
study I referred to as astronomical folklore a line of
inquiry as you might imagine that wasn't especially lucrative or
even well-regarded but I muddled through somehow
with a loose or not so loose strange how such matters can often be so fluid
and murky affiliation with a local and rather prestigious research
university and I did in fact manage to publish several
influential papers during that time and even one
well-received book an output that didn't strike me
as all that impressive while I was about it researching and

writing but that yes seems more meritorious now looking back on it though one of the more lasting and rewarding results if the truth be told was the extensive collection of Sun Ra records I amassed during that period and though his cosmology never made a lick of sense to me primarily because his was a constantly shifting scatterbrained philosophy which I doubt he himself understood much of the time other than recognizing his role as an entertainer acting out an ever-morphing decades-long piece of gripping theater so that his music took over without much of a fight I must admit my more erudite studies and I'd sit mesmerized by the hours listening letting my work my career such as it was slip away so much the better most likely and anyway it's simply a testament to the power of Ra's magic there was no reason to fight it better just to give up as I explained to a colleague at the time and let yourself swing through the cosmos

III

Soon after my first meeting with Angelika I traveled to a conference in Germany which I had been greatly anticipating prior to our meeting but which seemed less inviting subsequently almost a chore by the time I settled down in my seat on the airplane exasperated by the long security line in the airport and the great hassle as always of unloading unfastening undoing myself and all my belongings and laying them out on the conveyor belt to participate once again in that great mechanized acceptance ritual we've constructed for ourselves another compulsory plea for approval though I can't say whether my encounter with Angelika had any real connection to my loss of interest in the conference the truth is that I often experience a flush of excitement at the thought of a new undertaking but shortly thereafter feel the thrill begin to wane till I am more or less unsettled if not fully panicked or disgruntled or despondent by the time the event finally rolls around I had planned on presenting something or other when I first got word of the conference some yet formless wonder that would catapult me up the towers of academia but as the days and weeks flipped past I grew less enamored of such a project and soon came to hate not only the idea of presenting but to hate myself as well for ever having aspired to achieving such glory such nonsense by giving a show of flexed intelligence I doubted in fact whether I even or ever possessed the requisite intelligence to seem competent let alone brilliant the truth being that the ordeal of booking my flight and hotel and otherwise organizing my trip had taxed my brain to such an extent that I felt foolishly helpless in the face of it foolishly ill-equipped for the rigors of day-to-day adult life and that I might even collapse from the strain of it which would not have been an altogether unwelcome result

I returned to my apartment several days later to find a note posted on the door from Angelika instructing me to meet her at a nearby café that Saturday so we could in her words or word more accurately chat it was difficult to discern impossible in fact from this note how urgent a matter this was that is I couldn't sense whether Angelika was in some sort of trouble thinking back on it now knowing how everything ended it's rather impossible not to view it in a dark light but not to throttle myself unduly there was no reason at the time for my judgment to be clouded with such thoughts so likely I was simply more confused than anything with any anxiety injected not by her impending demise but by my worry over how she had acquired my address I certainly didn't recall giving her this information but had I only forgotten? an erasure in a block of my memory a possibility that left me standing there stupidly in front of my apartment door having not even unlocked the thing yet after having been away several days overseas worrying that this lapse in my memory could be a sign of a prematurely deteriorating brain I ran my hand through my hair I think and then unlocked the door peeling the note loose as I entered the apartment although in all likelihood I had already peeled the note from the door in order to read it but I entered the apartment nonetheless and then stood not but three paces inside the closed door still wearing my coat and read and reread the note trying to sort out how Angelika had found me how she had gained entrance to my building how long she had been following me from before our meeting at the velodrome? the nature of this requested meeting and whether or not it was wise to attend

IV

Sinatra should have recorded the third record of *Trilogy* with Sun Ra I told Angelika upon sitting down at the table outside the café not with Gordon Jenkins wouldn't that have been a gas? her brow crinkled just the slightest bit and the corners or was it just one corner of her mouth lifted conveying bemused indifference which she shook free of her head soon enough proclaiming looking down so it's gotten bad no? I looked at her silently perhaps brushing a thumb across my lips trying to appear concerned while also trying to divine from her manner from the fluid expressions redrawing her face the cause of her worry she looked up and said she was truly frightened now by what was occurring in Eastern Ukraine I even and here she fell silent again and turned her face away from me looking down at the pebbled concrete on which we and our table and our chairs rested it makes no sense I know she said then quietly I can't even rightly call the place mine but still I can't help feeling that I'm losing something very close to me and violently no less it's being ripped from me I nodded although in truth I couldn't yet appreciate her torment why the increased aggression of the pro-Russian separatists as they had come to be consistently called by the media had had such a profound effect on this woman who hadn't visited the place since her childhood and who couldn't even rightly recall the house of her grandfather in which she had spent those youthful summers still I had to confess and indeed thoughts of this weakness did run through my mind sitting there at the table that I had in my time harbored similar thoughts feelings for

Ireland although I had no direct connection to the place other than vague ancestral ties nevertheless there had been a time when my pulse would quicken at word of infractions committed by the British perhaps Klitschko will knock them all out I told her grinning although I'm not sure she picked up on my reference I having recalled seeing a brief notice in the paper about Wladimir Klitschko's recent KO victory over Alex Leapai in Germany to retain his heavyweight titles proclaiming glory to Ukraine! afterwards although just as likely she merely failed to see the humor in my comment and in fact may have taken my mention of the fight as an indication of my inability or lack of desire to empathize with her crisis I almost started using again she said an utterance made so quietly and without the slightest tenor of alarm that it nearly slipped past me unrecognized and I think I may have even begun to nod though the sense of this could easily have been assigned to the scene after the fact after I could look and couldn't help but look back upon it through the filter of all I was to learn later casually acknowledging her near miss without comprehending in the least what she was talking about till all of a sudden it hit me and I fairly blurted out heroin? which startled her to such an extent as to indicate that perhaps even she hadn't registered the severity of her almost slip until that very moment yes she confided hoarsely yes heroin after which she shook her head slowly and fell to considering her latte I had an overwhelming desire to reach out and take her hand but I refrained of course recognizing the absurdity of such a response the inappropriateness the foolishness so I sat still and simply watched her with a look no doubt of unhelpful pity on my face

Odessa was burning I believe or had burned one building of it anyway with no one quite knowing or perhaps caring which side was responsible for the blaze which claimed around 50 lives though regardless it was a troubling sign as the Black Sea port town of one million had seemed to erupt as if by spontaneous combustion or as if it were a release valve venting excess pressure from Eastern locales making it easy to imagine that the whole damn country might explode soon I have no idea how to feel anymore she said I guess I never did only that before the whole thing was less chaotic and frightening and it was easier to assume that my thoughts and feelings were together when in fact they were just less intense and manageable I recall her wiping her mouth then with a napkin causing a sudden break in her dialogue as if cleaning her lips of remaining words I felt I should reply in some fashion but my brain generated no substantive thoughts it did in fact become increasingly less plastic steadily hardening into a cement block so that I sat there stupidly uncomfortably looking at her hoping she might once again begin speaking shedding some light on the happenings in Ukraine some inside angle courtesy of her ancestry and childhood summers or better yet that she might change the subject completely and speak about less severe and depressing matters about us perhaps ha! it was the first I had thought of it or at least the first time I had thought about it in such a concrete manner the first I had caught myself thinking about it I must have begun smiling for she looked at me a bit queerly not unlike she had done when I mentioned the Sinatra/Sun Ra teaming or was it when I mentioned Klitschko and then suddenly I had the desire to tell her something about Gerry Adams and the renewed potential for violence in Northern Ireland now that he had been detained for questioning in relation to the murder of a Belfast woman in 1972 but just as I was about to part my lips and start in it occurred to me that I hadn't in fact said anything to her earlier about my inauthentic Republican fervor but had only thought it or more accurately I couldn't recall whether I had said anything to her or not an uncertainty that left me there squirming inside both over the troubling sensation of such immediate memory loss and the revulsion at having been and continuing to be to some extent that mindless nationalistic stooge and for a country that wasn't even mine no less she smiled sadly but warmly maybe we should talk about something else she said it's all quite ridiculous isn't it?

V

Later during our second round of coffee if memory serves we had a third that day as well but perhaps I am mistaken about that we got around to discussing the fate of the space station now that the US had leveled sanctions against Russia for their involvement in the disturbances in Eastern Ukraine and Russia had responded by indicating that is one of their responses was to indicate that it might no longer give US astronauts access to Russian launch vehicles thus effectively shutting the Americans off from the International Space Station the US having depended on Russian transportation since retiring its fleet of space shuttles

Russia's Deputy Prime Minister Dmitry Rogozin suggesting even that the Americans could shoot their astronauts to the space station with a trampoline Angelika shaking her head in disbelief while laughing another role for Sun Ra I said ah but he's no longer around Angelika reminding me true I said before correcting myself maybe Angelika sat back in her chair and looked at me smiling her eyes wide and also smiling her hair long and black and full draping down over her shoulders in easy waves the first and maybe only time I took notice of her hair or better that it made an impression on me you're a conspiracy theorist then? she kidded me the living Ra will return just you wait I told her

A rather lengthy silence followed this repartee I think till I said but no seriously it's too bad Ra is no longer around it would be interesting to hear his take on the return to Cold War-era space politics Angelika shrugged and looked away at something

Later she told me about her first experiences with heroin

VI

Space is the place he proclaimed waving us aboard
a mischievous grin threatening to win control of his cheeks
the ship was a flesh-colored Caucasian flesh that is
inflatable joke with two breast-like rockets holding
the cabin betwixt like a barbell the rockets' areolas
ringed with painted flames that streaked back over the
rounded burners in flamboyant hotrod fashion to lick the
rockets' pointed spermy tails we disappeared inside the
cabin's open snatch white smoke billowing forth from its
innards where Ra now settled in behind the keyboard
controls cranking his head back over his right regally

robed shoulder to call over the rising din of whirring dissonant space music something that sounded very much like throttle them tits! but it was impossible to say for sure if this was indeed what he said or not or if in fact his next words were burn em dry! but as we lifted from the grass and the roar of the engines subsided and the spaceship Judgment purred smoothly up through the atmosphere to a swinging velvet beat Ra spoke again and his words found easy passage to our ears crooning I am the altered destiny

Each of us nodded in unison though we hadn't the slightest idea what he was talking about besides myself there being a gangly woman with straw-colored hair probably in her early 20s a chocolate-skinned man who smelled like smoke or was it dust as Johnny Dowd might have it and another being not quite man or woman or both maybe morphing back and forth who most regularly evidenced a blazing purple skin that in the dimly lit spacecraft darkened into a sumptuous eggplant color that more than once drew my curious tongue to it corralling this fleshy being into some darkened corner where tiny amber lights flashed and machinery clicked like flickering insects to sample greedily with lick the firm curve of shoulder meat

Back behind Ra at the keys the four of us hovered anxiously which isn't to say that we were floating though perhaps come to think of it we were doing this too forming a quarter moon behind the rotation of the pianist's the keyboardist's the maestro's the leader's great swiveling chair he growled something now or maybe it's better to say that his lips his throat fashioned a continual hum his large powerful hands stroking the array of keys releasing a highly pleasant cacophony of squelching bird calls rendered metallic and thundering drum noises though his hands in truth never touched the keys but skimmed just above on a slick sliver of air time is officially ended! he declared though the swing never faltered nor lost its beat

The black passenger struck up a match his skin going suddenly chalky semi-sweet though I had not to the best of my knowledge actually sampled the flavor of his flesh but rather had intuited it as he gave scent to the skin of his cigar a juicy leaf that incensed the spacious cockpit's otherwise ozone-inflamed environs mixed with heated Cold War-era metal cabinetry green the heavy odor of cured tobacco smoke curling neath our noses for an effect not at all unpleasant but put that monstrosity out! Sun Ra chimed nonetheless tis earthly malfeasance to which the smoking man just chuckled and continued puffing away the girl for young she did appear at this passage though later there would be nothing youthful about her all whitewashed and wrinkled began to furiously stroke her long well-lined crinkly hair just how far out are we going? she asked in something of a frantic whisper her already alluringly wide-set eyes drawing yet farther away from one another till the expanse wholly filled my vision and she softened you'll see Ra said simply or something akin to that which put us all at ease and we sat or leaned rather back in luxuriant comfort as the good or bad ship Judgment streaked through the darkest endless hole of space passing planets and other rocks like creamy comets swimming

the cosmos with energetic swishing of jelly tails going
indeed farther out farther still escaping the tight
restraining wires of existence

The planet Earth of course is coming to an end Ra
declared his right hand jumping about on the high end
of his keyboard cutting loose a series of icy sharp
block chords that conjoined in the ear and froze over
the next stretch of his speech I tried to warn the people the
humans but there wasn't anyone who wanted to hear they
just kept on defiling the creation not recognizing it as
creation but rather as something eternal that couldn't go away as
something they had inherited and would forever be I came
and tried to tell them but they wouldn't listen couldn't listen
being humans themselves so the destruction was inevitable and
nobody wanted to hear that either but became mired remained
mired for it was always thus in the myth of their inconsequential
existences but it has come to pass just the same the ice
thawing loose now regardless of belief and the people
are scattering flailing sinking moaning and gnashing
teeth with the destruction that I bespoke but that
nobody back then wanted to hear

The woman for she had aged considerably now had by

this time tugged all but the last few strands of straw from her head the remaining few adopting a thin feathery quality that caused them to curl back toward her scalp with even a few pieces becoming intertwined and knotting together at the ends she slipped two fingers into one such loop now and tore it loose from her head in a furious fit of aggression ain't nothing that will take away the pain of ignorance and Earth-bound anti-enlightenment Sun Ra said almost to himself the delicious purple creature turning a most enlightened green at this point exuding a sticky plant-like warning that stung our nostrils with harsh reference to Earth's soiled exuberance

My ear was close to Ra's lips then whether through my own volition or directed hence by Ra himself I can no longer recall if indeed I ever knew and he was whispering a voice that recalled the high-warp rev of a vacuum cleaner if quieted and slowed considerably she will be expiring he said in a tone both sad and accepting and I immediately thought of Angelika though I can't say for sure now if his words preceded or followed her death I was struck by an overwhelming feeling of loss of irreparable tearing sadness the black passenger whose chalky skin was sweating now while strangely disturbingly remaining rough and dry to the touch offered me a drag from his smoke which became new on my lips and had to be relit a match struck to his dry chuckle and I was inhaling a pound of pressurized smoke that nearly cut off my breath she's expiring whispered Sun Ra close at my ear and I nodded accepting hurting swallowing smoke a deep red burned out from my chest quickly coloring warming my arms till they radiated with an almost unbearable heat a deep-bone itch that tickled up through my forearms rode the humeri to put scraping fingers in my throat I know it I said and Sonny looked very stern but relieved

Later when the straw-haired woman had pulled her last and lay dead on the scuffed cross-hatching of the spacecraft's steel floor her quiet face locked in a grimace of struggle I got hold of a broom and was futilely sweeping about her head the scratch of the broom's bristles not only failing to corral the ship's detritus but in fact seeming to create more of it till silt and gravel were being brushed uncontrollably into the corpse's ears and wrenched-open mouth stop! I commanded my arms but they continued sweeping with a weak jelly inevitability a last uncontrollable stroke gouging deep red lacerations into the corpse's right cheek and I tossed the broom aside and refused to look

I think he might very well be mad the black man said his cigar stretching thin and long now and glowing at its tip a perfectly circular smokeless orange LED to the apparent delight of the purple creature who hummed a deep warm pleasure its quite rotund bulbous body pressing to full expression engorging likewise my loins to my horror so that I pleaded silently with the force to stop expanding but lost all restraint in the licentious smile of the glad beast who could withhold no more and popped my come pumping freely in a showering goo that nonetheless evaporated in the moment of consideration glad I was to discover that no one else in the craft had noticed if indeed any of this had even happened

There's no need to worry Sun Ra said from his command post at the starship's controls which had been diminished perhaps by his weight perhaps by the vacuum pull of space to a deeply compressed tiny keyboard resting precariously on his large thighs his mouth opening as if to speak some ultimate reassurance

VII

Coffee is a poor substitute she said for the really
big rush of injection of the junk a comical emphasis
placed on the word junk leaning forward and smiling
for a reason that wasn't entirely clear to me whether
through discomfort or instead a well-earned comfort that
allowed or compelled her to mock the substance that had
previously won her or maybe she had come to see it as
a worthy adversary a despoiler that wrecked lives
through no great fault of its own only that its powerful
hands were crude and clumsy an intended soft caress

striking down like a boulder a kiss smacking a head like granite and so after wriggling free of it Angelika came to regard heroin more as a once lover who didn't work out who caused her great grief and turmoil and loss but only because the two of them were not made for each other heroin after all wasn't evil it just wasn't compatible with her or most likely with anybody else but good times were had that couldn't be denied and memories of its sweet full-body comfort still lingered and probably always would she thought of heroin with a wistful fondness

Or maybe she didn't regard it in any such way and was simply messing around laughing at junk so as not to appear too serious so as not to be seen as a morose loser fishing for pity but when she gripped her mug again and brought it by a smooth strongly mechanical rotation of arm to her lips drinking with a disquieting deliberateness I saw which is to say I surmised that the need within her was still great that she still needed or sensed that she needed the quick chemical zap to stave off doom to quell the rioting spiders of hopelessness though or maybe because of her dose her lips relaxed into a gentle smile that calmed her eyes as well and I found myself quickly dismissing my thoughts from seconds earlier which is a romantic way of saying that my thoughts went away or left me even certainly I had not sent them out and Angelika became again a welcome comfort wholly substantive and warm and glowing

VIII

The gas light came on outside the shuttered windows
casting a peach block of light against the building's
stucco wall on the far side of the pond that lay before
the rectangular house with the tall green shutters Angelika
sat regarding it with a warm inner breeze of comfort her
legs sharply bent and laid to the side in the grass with
the right leg covering the left her left arm angled
straight from the heel of her palm propping her torso
upright while twisted at the hips so it was facing the house
her grandfather sat beside her most likely perhaps with

two or three of his friends and a bottle or two or three of white wine their happy chatter and laughter echoing off the house and trees still water and low clouds seemingly in a language she didn't understand save for the occasional word or two but it made her feel very much at home nonetheless

Occasionally she'd sense something like fingers on her skin the forearms mostly the fingernails soothingly scratching and awakening her flesh in long smooth strokes although her hands remained softly folded in her lap she sat contentedly watching the house its bright reflection of the streetlamp seeming also to brighten the night sky to daytime blue huge cumulus clouds hovered over the house nearly scraping in Angelika's imagination the large maple that stood in front of the house next to the streetlamp

Everything was quite sleepy and as her eyes drowsed the sky grew increasingly blue lightening that is rather than darkening as the time of day should dictate the night sky shimmering daylight over a darkening house Angelika sat up and blinked deliberately trying to resurrect herself but the sky only grew brighter casting a misty haze onto the night street as if a broad swath of transparent muslin had been draped over her grandfather's house its weave now inviting her eyelids to droop more heavily till she soon could no longer differentiate between the threads in the sky and those in the fabric of her eyelids the separation perhaps existing in a flickering of shadows like the projection of an old home movie the toggling between sleep and waking the lamp now lighting on a pack of large red feathers carried along atop a wide-brimmed hat bobbing up and down as the woman lower still beneath the feathers sauntered along the road by the lake her darkly colored feather boa perhaps also red tossing about with her stride her exposed skin about the face and hands was tight to the bone skeletal in appearance though perhaps it was only the strange light that gave this appearance or maybe that masked an even darker truth that in fact the woman was but a skeleton walking the night dead street laughing now with a scratched masculine timbre and then beginning to speak Ukrainian till her voice was overtaken by a boisterous guffaw loosed from the grandfather's throat and followed by an additional flow of

Ukrainian words that got caught up in phlegm and further laughter and coughing

Angelika turned to her grandfather hoping to divine from the mere presence of his body the glimmer in his eyes what in fact he was laughing about with his friends the content of his speech of course lost upon her but there in the daytime haze of that alien night her grandfather himself had advanced to the world of the dead evidencing a starkly raw yet nonetheless jovial skull the eye sockets dark and hollow above the empty and surprisingly small triangular hole that had once served as base for the old man's majestic nose his naked smile seeming oddly enough no broader than it had in life although was he not still living? still moving? still smiling and talking? you'll note my bare appearance he chuckled as if responding to these questions which she didn't believe she had put to voice it's sleeker if nothing else he said Angelika tried to maintain a smile but her cheeks were trembling her grandfather patted her hand we're all dying he assured her then he gave a long slow sweep to the sky with his left arm all this is dying and indeed the sky darkened several degrees as if poisoned by some spell cast through the arcing of her grandfather's arm with everything returning to normal then

IX

Iraq was at that time erupting again in violence with Sunni militants seizing major cities in the north of the country including Mosul the Shiite-led government forces simply laying down arms and abandoning the theater in the face of the coming onslaught leading some to suspect collusion with the insurgents from the Islamic State of Iraq and Syria which didn't make a whole lot of sense given the religious divide and was probably more a reflection of poor discipline and training and lack of equipment and ammunition some were saying and little to no investment by the troops or citizens in general in the government's agenda and any hope for a better future an unwillingness to be maimed or killed or to maim or kill others for the purpose of maintaining an order that didn't look too different than the one the opposition hoped to install especially when considering just the day-to-day existences of everyday people although ISIS had proclaimed in a 2007 pamphlet that improving the conditions of the citizens under their control was less important than ensuring the condition of a person's religion and perhaps verifying and exterminating if the condition of a given subject's religion wasn't up to snuff? already during their first days in Mosul they had summarily executed some police officers and government workers deemed criminals under the freshly established Islamic rule of law so all this weighed on my mind as I prepared to meet Angelika for dinner one Saturday evening in what was I suppose our first official date although neither of us called it that at the time and I can't say for certain if I even considered it as such or only attached that significance if significance can rightly be ascribed to such social encounters after the fact looking back but it would be false to say that I wasn't nervous that afternoon so I obviously attached some significance to the event and had a fear of failing to live up to some ill-defined social performance standard and thus blowing a fine opportunity to secure romantic companionship which of course is compulsory and desirable and then that same afternoon I learned of the latest violence in Ukraine with the pro-Russian separatists shooting down a Ukrainian military plane killing all 49 people aboard and of course greatly increasing tensions in the region compounded by the accusations by Ukraine the US NATO and others that Russia had indeed allowed or actively employed the transportation of three tanks across the border into Ukraine presenting aerial photos as evidence which Moscow of course dismissed while making their own claims of border violation twice by air and once by ground when a Ukrainian armored vehicle supposedly veered 500 feet into Russian territory so I feared not only my performance that evening while to be sure hating the cultural norms that placed such performance burdens upon me but also Angelika's emotional and mental state if indeed she had learned of this latest attack by the separatists which I felt safe in assuming she had although not without allowing myself the luxury of considering the possibility of her ignorance which perked me up for a moment or two thinking the evening might not be clouded by far-off war after all until I realized that as a carrier of this news I would be put into the position of deciding whether or not to tell her about it which of course seemed a ridiculous thing to do at first blush but would I be able to enjoy the evening holding back information that Angelika would no doubt like to have even if it made her sad or angry or what and what would happen if I didn't tell her and she found out later which she would and asked had I heard and I would either say yes or no but surely indicate or imply that I had not in fact known at the time of our dinner which would be a lie and would weigh on me along with the initial refusal to trust her with the information that is valuing my own chance at an enjoyable evening over her desire to hear news on an issue that was important to her my keeping it from her and my lying about it would weigh on me as great moral failings even if they were in the great order of things very inconsequential matters

We met rather early if memory serves around five o'clock or so at a casual falafel joint I patronized with some frequency the casual nature of the place again leading me to believe that neither of us was thinking of this dinner as a date the proprietor greeting me as I entered saying he hadn't seen me in a while although I thought it hadn't been all that long since my last visit a month or two maybe which amongst his cast of regular patrons was I suppose a considerable absence Angelika was seated at a table in the middle of the restaurant waiting for me she smiled warmly upon seeing me a look that immediately assured me that she had not heard the latest troubling news from Ukraine an assurance that just as quickly vanished as rational thought retook my mind reminding me that one might look warmly upon another even while holding dire thoughts in her mind I can't believe I've never been here she said as I sat down across from her and all my worry melted in her authentic excitement and we had as far as I can recall a completely enjoyable dinner in which none of the world's troubles was discussed which probably isn't

an accurate recollection of the evening for we must
have made mention of some and probably many
happenings and situations outside of our own personal realm
but still there was nothing that caused any agitation and from
that evening on we saw a great deal of one another

X

It was around that time that the Republican National Committee announced it would be holding its upcoming convention in our town which produced a cynical glint in Angelika's eye a cynicism that nonetheless sparkled with a certain criminal glee I can't believe they'd allow nay court that kind of bullshit here she told me motherfucking Republicans we need to grab em by the balls while they're here grab em by the balls and twist them off perform abortions on public square or something

something to really flip their wigs I laughed but without any degree of confidence that Angelika was joking there seemed in fact to be a heat radiating from her that signaled some kind of outside menace one perhaps that had swept in on the wave of fascistic tidings to take possession of our friend Angelika it struck me with both fear and excitement to see her so charged I'm sure you'll be able to get your fill of protests I said which immediately ignited a new rage in Angelika flashing across her face like shadow and light play from the clouds I don't just want some protest I recall her nearly screaming but probably she wasn't so aggressive in her response I want to be part of something that matters not comfortable continuing this line of talk with Angelika in such a state or with my imagining that she was in such a state I assured her that she would come up with something with the convention still two years off she certainly had enough time to develop a plan although just the thought of what monstrosity she might in fact unleash upon our fair city prevented me from relaxing any and I began to craft my own plan for excusing myself from Angelika that afternoon or morning or whatever it was with the hope that her rage at the announcement of the convention would pass over leaving her more sensible for our next encounter a parade of elephants tattooed with corporate logos ridden by geriatric white guys with unnaturally strong erections trampling people mostly women in the city streets she was musing as I was getting up and saying goodbye the people I suppose would have to be dummies though she conceded

XI

Not a single terrorist will avoid responsibility Poroshenko vowed after the rebel attack on a military camp in the Eastern Ukrainian town of Zelenopillya and Angelika felt compelled to guarantee that each of these terrorists would get what they deserved as the president had concluded so arriving in Luhansk she quickly outfitted herself in a full-skirted white embroidered number that she hoped would allow her quite apart from blending in to take on a certain air of conspicuous vacationing to strike something of a comical figure the tourist trying too hard that would put any notion of radical motives beyond consideration it was quite possible she had to admit that she had overthought the situation and indeed her traditional and thus ostentatious garb simply called unnecessary attention to her foreign body which in any event would be conspicuous simply by being in Eastern Ukraine at that time weaponry was more difficult to come by but in the end not as difficult as a person a middle-class American that is might think and after some haggling and venturing into backroom locales by ducking neath burlap drapery or slipping down ridiculously not to mention creepily narrow passages she found herself in bountiful stockrooms of armament staffed by exceedingly helpful patient attendants who discreetly determined her needs and sent her on her way with a compact automatic rifle a pistol and an exquisitely embossed yet conservative leather pouch filled with ammo

Out in the wilds then lumbering through deep tangles of forest she found herself wondering wandering if she had perhaps made a mistake but this self-doubt lasted only a moment or two yet enough time to etch her memory for later consideration she emerged from

the thicket ducking low then leaping from her crouch to
clear a hedgerow and traipsed on across a picnic
blanket with her rifle at the ready happy in her skill
at not disturbing the late afternoon diners on over
mounds of dirt and scattered rubble facing harsh
winds and rain later coming finally to an outlying
shack that sat alone at a barely visible crossroads
the wooden sign nailed above the ill-fitted door
declaring the place as Ye Olde Forty-niner which
didn't strike her as odd until she had already turned open the
door which felt at first as if it were going to fall loose in her hands
but then hung steady solidly though on a heavily awkward
slant coming into the place that was surprisingly full
if still free of a great number of patrons owing to the
small size of the joint the weathered heads creased
hatted and spiked by a stubble of beards lifted to inspect
her entrance and at first spark ignited in surprise but just
as quickly went blank again and returned to the pale beer
in their greasy glass steins or the greasy aperitifs in their
pale diminutive glass vases and to their rough-edged
conversations that cut a rumbling everyday static beneath
the drifting fog of cigarette smoke Angelika went

straight to the bar and without hesitation in a fluid twist of shoulder unburdened herself of her weapon propping it smartly against the side of the bar as she took up a stool and with a knowing nod of her chin ordered up a doll-sized glass of her own filled to the rim with some oily blaze of local magic

He came up and sat next to her sometime later the fingers of his left hand fully enmeshed in the curls of his thick black beard knitting away like a caffeinated spider albeit without the result of spinning anything new you stick out like a sore thumb he said continuing to stare forward at the shelves behind the bar which were mostly empty save for a handful of bottles some of which likewise were empty she didn't attempt a reply but sat still and waited for him to say something more

I can help he said finally who says I'm looking for help? was her adroit but too ready reply he chuckled though still refused to look in her direction it doesn't need to be said he told her it can be taken for granted though no doubt you are unaware of this yourself she smirked producing along with twisted lips a dismissive guttural noise which she acknowledged to herself was several degrees less than convincing and she ended up leaving with the man sometime later

Pressed after the fact she was at pains to recount the series of events that brought her over the ensuing weeks to a remote village near the Luhansk-Donetsk border waking one morning inside a pungent earth-scented sleeping bag to news of a downed aircraft and discussion over the wisdom of fleeing or staying put and once out of the bag and up on her feet the eyes of others in the group either looked askance upon passing or avoided her form altogether she didn't know what it all meant but was glad to find that she was not rejected when the band collected and began to march out though still no one would speak to her or look much in her direction she searched as best she could the faces of the others but failed to find the thickly bearded man she had met in the bar how many days or weeks earlier she still carried the rifle which felt at this point like a natural extension of her arm though it startled her to see it there nonetheless and wondered if the others simply hadn't noticed it either otherwise surely they would have taken it away from her she felt without knowing why but then everyone had a weapon at least one so maybe no infraction was severe enough to be punishable by the revocation of arms an actual arm would sooner be cleft off she had a feeling than taking away one's weapon after all what would you use then to kill others? still she couldn't say what she had done or even why she had the prevailing feeling of having done anything and not just anything but something critically damning to herself and the movement as a whole critically damning and irrevocable visions of firing a surface-to-air missile till she recalled that she had no idea not only how to fire a surface-to-air missile but that she had no idea even what a surface-to-air missile or more correctly the firing apparatus for a surface-to-air missile looked like still the vision of firing the missile indeed the feeling of doing so remained fresh and vital in her mind and body and later the jetliner screamed to the earth in a bright bending arc I am not a terrorist though she reminded herself I came here to fight for the state which made her just as uncomfortable when she said it

XII

I think I've seen that boy before Angelika said a bemused twist to her lips or have I not? she shook her head slowly then back and forth smiling if I'm not mistaken we had a date or two driven by this unlikely scenario I turned to check out the male barista myself which upon seeing him set my head to shaking too no I told her I've never seen him before well why would you? she chuckled you never went on a date with him how do you know? I mused turning back to look at the boy as Angelika had labeled him for want of a proper name in fact yes I think we did in fact have a date or two during my experimenting days you understand Ed! she blurts Ed? no hmmmmm her lips crowding into her left cheek maybe not of course not nobody's called Ed anymore somebody must be no nobody hmmmm I guess not but really if you went on a date with him surely you'd remember maybe I go on a lot more dates than you she grinning I don't doubt it but still she shrugs all boys look more or less the same anyway so you gonna start calling me Ed now too? maybe her right forefinger pointing at me in pistol fashion the thumb collapsing on top of it as she says if you're not careful my hands come up belatedly POW! no you're right she says later I never dated him but the sense of familiarity is disturbing maybe you knew someone else named Ed she considers it hmmmm I don't think so but maybe

XIII

I was alone I think when I heard about Michael
Brown but by alone I mean I was in a crowd of people at a
coffee shop tapping away at some inanity on my
computer trying to look busy and of course failing miserably
which is to say intentionally grazing the Internet and I came
across a notice of the boy's shooting which at first I admit had
little to no effect on me another shooting yes? and it wasn't
until later that it began to drill into me that this might
be a moment of some significance a moment that
might cause things to change and a few days later
Angelika and I went downtown to join in the local

moment of silence and protest and both put our
hands up a number of times it seems and hollered don't
shoot! and posed and were shot by cameras there was
a general excitement and late evening exhaustion
propelling us home to our various spots about town
shot like arrows as it were in authoritative directions and
when we went to bed that night or at least when I went to
bed that night I was fueled by this compelling reason
for action and it took me a long time to drift off to sleep

XIV

I woke up in the middle of the street with a heavy
rain shooting sideways such was the angle of the
downpour in fact that it failed mostly in getting me wet if
I stayed low enough huddled in my sleeping bag but it was
time to get up anyway and Angelika was hailing me
from a pickup parked nearby at an angle perpendicular
to that struck by me and my bag her headlights but a yard or
two away from my toes the truck apparently having
served as her lodging for the night and now she was
waving me over to get out of the rain and join her in

proper shelter and probably to accompany her to breakfast somewhere so indeed I got up and went over to her with my bag and began rolling it up only then thinking on how dangerous it was to have spent the night sleeping in the middle of the street and on how lucky I was to have escaped the episode unscathed and on how my lack of concern or recognition more correctly of the danger was what had allowed me to sleep peacefully through the night though there wasn't to be sure much traffic on that street ever

XV

The priest made the appropriate hand motions and mumblings before the truck then went around to the passenger side and climbed in with the trucks rumbling forward then across the border in a strong white line of rattling obstinate defiance critical humanitarian aid the Russians say thinly veiled invasion the Ukrainians say half empty fully empty partially full cargo trucks knocking down the main road to Luhansk then turning off and heading north via country road into the village of Uralo-Kavkaz to avoid

Ukrainian troops coming some 80 years after the Holodomor which is still widely a secret the genocide of millions unmentioned in the West coming into Ukraine this time instead of hauling people wasted out to Siberia and other desolate locales leaving them to scavenge fruitlessly for food and evaporate into the frozen air the trucks now a ruse to provide cover for pro-Russian separatists who were on the point of being overrun by Ukrainian forces the white Russian trucks a dare as it were to the Ukrainian government to continue military action against the rebels and thereby risk striking these mobile offerings of humanitarian aid

Bullshit Angelika pronounces Putin will say anything to advance his imperialistic aims or to keep the rest of the world from stopping him more accurately he's mimicking Stalin and the world sits by and watches forgets and watches

XVI

Cease-fire my ass Angelika grumbled as I sat down at her table she was holding a newspaper off to the side of the table in outstretched arms who the fuck do they think they're kidding? I didn't say a word I smiled I might have shrugged but this obviously wasn't the response she was looking for and she went back to her reading for a while when she spoke again it was a recitation of numerals 8 19 9 2 9 13 followed by a shaking of her head I looked at her straight annoyed I shrugged this time I'm sure of it triggering a quick flashing of her eyes caught annoyance or better an allergic reaction an ocular histamine to combat my annoyance then she said expanding her eyes still further the beheadings? I shook my own head gently enough that I had no fear of it breaking loose she sighed and turned back to her paper in Iraq she said in a calmer tone or wherever they're doing it her eyes scanning the outstretched pages before her and after a spell in which apparently she'd found nothing said ISIL otherwise known as ISIS or the Islamic State I added grinning and she turned my way and smiled too you're quite a peculiar person aren't you? I shrugged again annoying myself now with the limited repertoire I felt stuck in she folded up her paper and set it aside on the table she leaned forward her forearms lined against one another beneath her supporting her upper body and preventing it from toppling over what are we doing? she asked in a suddenly pleasant inviting purr we're looking to eat some breakfast I said turning away as if for the waiter no she said her hand on my forearm now are we as they say an item? who are these people that are talking about us? I asked no one she replied unfazed the line of her lips seeming to lengthen and twist up slightly at the ends her hand on my arm seeming to tighten its grip or increase the warmth of its pressure though quite likely this was all only a product of my perception it's 9_{18} time for you to decide she smiled truly now do you want to be left alone? yes or no? I looked at her for a long time after that the waiter may even have come and we may have consulted our menus and placed our orders and maybe even begun to discuss other things or maybe it was a long second or two I don't think I placed my hand on hers on top of my forearm before I relented and breathed and said no

XVII

I say relented but that may not be fair or accurate rather
for was I really giving in to something? something I
didn't really want? I still can't say to be honest I
wanted to be with Angelika of course and in fact I
was with her whether it was up to that point labeled
something or other or not and truth be told it was not
labeled anything even after that point at least I never
considered it to be and I don't recall her ever pronouncing
anything of the sort but surely after that point it was
proper to proceed with the understanding that

something had indeed been decided like when you choose your way along a path that forks you don't call it anything you simply go one way or another and any labels that might be applied to the course come only after the fact and usually only if you walk that way often and there becomes some meaning some rightly partitioned recollection to taking one path over another each having its own character and over the course of time a collection of memories associated with moving in that direction is compiled so that grouping them under some heading filing them in some folder as it were seems proper if not necessary to help us manage all the exploding minutia of our lives is constructing such order formulating such constructs tantamount to giving in to something? is it conforming? losing yourself? I don't know I only know that it often feels as such like betrayal betrayal against the self like an opportunity lost instead of gained an opportunity to choose all other opportunities cast aside in favor of locking yourself onto this one particular individual distinct rail

that might not offer any quick or even delayed exit on
the horizon I don't know I've been told that I'm
too cautious too scared and it's hard to argue against
such assessments but admitting accepting these
diagnoses does nothing it seems to shield me from
destruction

XVIII

The bombs rained down on the town of Qourieh near Syria's border with Turkey but they weren't exactly serious strikes so said Redur Xelil spokesman for the People's Protection Units also known as the YPG a group of Kurdish fighters in Syria adding that if the US and its allies were serious then the YPG also known as the People's Protection Units would be willing to cooperate but ohhhh that be problematic since Turkey's Kurdistan Workers' Party also known as the PKK is designated a terrorist group by Turkey also known as the United States and by the United States also known as Turkey and there is little trust by Turkey of its Kurdish population so the refugees continue to stream into Turkey from the Syrian town of Ayn al-Arab also known as Kobani and Kurdish fighters amass in Kobani also known as Ayn al-Arab to defend the Kurdish region against an ISIS also known as ISIL also known as the Islamic State advance for a spokesman for the Islamic State also known as ISIS also known as ISIL and even sometimes known as Daesh has proclaimed that the strikes on Qourieh were in fact for naught the brothers have taken a new path he said they decided to change the way they operate it's almost impossible to know where the brothers are they disappeared they became ghosts their heavy weapons disappeared and they slipped ever closer to Ayn al-Arab once also known as Kobani

XIX

It was around this time that I suddenly became frightened that Angelika was getting too close I can't say what caused my retreat into self for that's essentially what I did for several weeks most likely there was no great cause no singular offensive by Angelika that struck me as too encroaching too dear the fact being that I had over many years developed a certain reticence to communing with others of opening myself up to them and even of allowing them the space to open themselves up to me I didn't want to know it was a responsibility I didn't want to shoulder after all dealing with myself managing my own problems was usually more than I could handle more than I wanted to handle which no doubt would lead many to argue that for this very reason I should in fact open myself up to others let them take some of the load that mutual sharing served to relieve tension and angst in both parties but sharing took more than I could muster was more than I could stomach I always detested it so when Angelika suggested that we go to Toronto for a long weekend together I immediately rejected the idea making some lame and baldly transparent excuse about being too busy the disappointment immediately apparent on her face a transparency that further drove my instinct to shrink back but she said it was fine she understood which of course she did her correct understanding being that I wished to pull away from her thus shredding a previous understanding which to be sure I had cultivated that I wished to advance our closeness I should have left it at that but feeling suddenly culpable for her disappointment for betraying her in a sense I belabored the point continuing to talk on in an effort to explain in detail and hopefully legitimize my claim of justifiable busyness but the more I went on the less believable my claim became the legitimacy of the excuse monitored with great accuracy by Angelika's expression a meter inescapably signaling my lie back to me like one of those electronic speed monitoring signs that flashes your often law-breaking speed at you in large shaming red numerals which isn't to say that Angelika was flushed at all but still the transformation of her expression as I spoke its evolving message its evolving condemnation was just as clear as if she had become beet red I mumbled my way to a conclusion and she nodded repeatedly saying OK OK I gave a weak smile which I immediately regretted and later or precisely at that moment Angelika got up and walked away from the table

XX

I entered the café and sat down at my usual table usual being relative of course since usual can represent a daily choice a weekly one monthly yearly what have you depending on the person and the activity at hand Ed was supposed to be coming but there was always some question of whether he would show or not whether he'd remember and be on time he was rarely on time some last-minute quirk could flip him or his mind leastways 180° and you wouldn't see him then for who knows how long and always without notice which got to be less of a hassle less unpredictable once you got to know him so I'd sit and wait for a while then get up and leave when the time was right this day he arrived rather timely actually presenting himself in quite a jovial mood or what passed as jovial for Ed the deficit in his mood being so great from the start that any uptick might be registered as jovial though the same mood in others might well be viewed as depression at least mildly he even took my hands which were resting on the table I think maybe not and from that point we chatted amicably and I recall the afternoon as an altogether pleasant one filled with laughter and even complex and meaningful conversation so that when I left when we parted I was gripped by the unshakeable sense that we would through mutual if unspoken agreement be quite inseparable for some time to come

XXI

I found Dottie's one night running up Lee Rd in the
rain sprinting laughing wildly for no reason after an
evening drinking at Parnell's with a friend as I recall
Dottie's had not been our destination all at once my
friend simply became stricken by the desire to see her old high
school there one block north and we started running shortly
thereafter she in front me in chase collapsing into one
another in fits of laughter several minutes later on the
corner of Lee & Washington which might also be
thought of as Washington & Lee the name the auto repair

shop there took and continues to hold the rain thrashing down so that our hair seemed to be pouring off our heads in slick threaded sheets of water flowing and it was hard to keep our eyes open I took off running again I think or maybe she did as I said with no destination which was madly intoxicating over and above the Guinness we'd ingested sliding at some points as it seems to me running downhill and there after a while we came upon Dottie's Diner and dashed in so it was with a certain nostalgic bite that I learned of the fire that consumed The Katz Club or part of it anyways which was owned by Doug Katz a man known primarily for his other restaurant Fire ironically enough nearly ten years after the former eatery had closed up shop in the same if remodeled diner cars The Katz Club the bar portion of the establishment that is the part gutted by the fire was a 1952 boxcar model built in Atlantic City while the 1949 Katz Diner portion originally known as Sweet City Diner when it was brought to town in 2002 from Berwick PA where it had gone quite belovedly apparently by the name Zephyr Diner remained at least in the initial reports salvageable so there was in those days after the early morning October fire the hope yet of another rebirth for the spot which had exchanged various owners and names over the years Favor Bistro most recently before Katz which in fact seemed so ill-favored that it never even got around to putting up a proper sign Clyde's before that which indeed had been quite popular and was the only other incarnation besides Dottie's that I experienced firsthand which is to say where I had actually eaten and before that several years before Chris & Jimmy's which I only know from the news reports after the fire although it was open longer than any of the others three years apparently named after and run by two brothers and their father ghosts now spirited away in the smoke that billowed up Lee Rd in the pre-light hours of that October morn to disappear into a community's recollection or lack thereof

XXII

I was pleased to see Modiano awarded the Nobel for I
had just discovered him myself earlier that year or perhaps
at the end of the previous year happening upon a copy of
Out of the Dark at a library book sale if they had held onto
the book for another year 10 months even would they ever have
parted with it? and then after reading and enjoying it its slow
melancholic intensity which made me long more so than ever to be lost
telling a friend about it only to discover that she too
owned one of his books Night Rounds which I
borrowed and also enjoyed for its confusion of characters
and their relation to one another and the eventual if not

complete discovery on both fronts if not as much as Out of
the Dark for it didn't leave me with the same nostalgic
feel for a past that wasn't my own but should have been

XXIII

With the truce waning in Ukraine I was feeling more and more of a pull to return not to my grandfather's house although I admit when I thought of returning the old house invariably glowed in my mind but to join the fight wherever it might be the separatists had taken or were close to taking or had been repelled from the Donetsk Airport which seemed like a key strategic position although to be honest I can't say whether it really was or not but with the rise of ISIS and Ebola and to be fair a dampening of violence in Ukraine only 331 had died since the truce was struck a little more than a month earlier the world which is to say the West had largely lost sight of Ukraine and the continued push by the separatists and their Russian accomplices to not only hold onto the gains they'd achieved through the months of fighting but to take new land and hold that too even now as they were working their way toward control of the airport the separatists were calling for a return to peace the strategy was obvious claw away preferably in fits of action the airport attack was one of 35 launched by the rebels within a 24-hour period at Ukrainian positions gain what they could quickly then throw up their hands demanding peace thereby inching their way toward conquest of the East as the world sat idle or at best occupied with other matters happy it seems to me to have excuses to ignore the troubles in Ukraine the troubles with Russia and Putin although to be fair the West seemed not to want to be bothered by much of anything ISIS Syria Africa Ebola global climate change economic inequality corporate rule and human misery generally misery was only a campaign vehicle a way to get elected after that it was back to leather sofas tumblers of Scotch and covert sexual infidelities and the poor fuckers of the world and the world itself be damned I had to go back it seemed now beyond question but that would mean sacrificing other things other pleasures other commitments Ed would have to be done away with which sounded rather violent when phrased in that manner criminal but there was no pretending that it didn't need to be done even as I fought for rationale to keep it going he could go with me! but even halfway through that thought I knew it was silly he barely had interest in talking about Ukraine he certainly was not inclined toward action action in any regard for any reason or cause I must sadly admit now so I had to break it off I told myself while still harboring thoughts of simply slipping away without a word which would be the simplest thing to do but probably wasn't right I didn't want to be plagued later by weaseling out now so a clean cut was best to behead the monster

XXIV

Somehow or for some reason rather I let slip to Ed that
I had notions of going to Ukraine which sent him not
unexpectedly for a loop although what was surprising
was the reason learned after some back and forth some give
and take for his concern you'd travel under these
delicate conditions? he'd asked what delicate
conditions? I'm not pregnant if that's what you're
on about? no his head shaking vigorously utterly
annoyed at my admittedly incongruous inappropriate by
his leveling interjection Ebola he practically shouted

his eyes expanding at the same time mine were rolling back into their lids you're kidding right? Ebola? I have more chance catching pregnancy on the plane which he seemed immediately to dismiss as pompous buffoonery but then showed concern over recognizing the implication well do what you want he said finally clearly distraught and exhausted and we didn't talk anymore about it

XXV

The window was pebbled with moisture as I awoke the sky thick and gray beyond dimensionless miles above the Earth the steady hum of the jets sealing the high atmospheric pressure in my head as if duct tape had been wrapped several times tightly about my skull covering the ears in sticky confinement I settled back and closed my eyes several times trying to convince myself that it was acceptable to surrender once again to sleep but each time being nagged by the insistence to do something the horrors of accomplishment that pulled me around finally to sitting upright and focusing my eyes blinking now with determined purpose to get down to work and start laying out my plan of action for when I deplaned which I had only slightly considered vague dreamlike notions of the course I would follow which seems completely improper immature and was but I was loath to draw a map the mere thought of which only served to drag me down into ponds of depression so I had skipped it but crunch time was nearing now and I could no longer avoid making some kind of concrete plan drumming up not only the insistence but the means of joining the fight how I could become as they say entrenched and then some an active participant and not just a monitor a reporter a hanger-on but a fighter which had been my intention I suppose whether I knew it at the time or not ever since I had heard of the struggle of the protests the violence the murder in Maidan Nezalezhnosti in February I couldn't just go back to sleep

XXVI

There I was a woman in a crowded foreign airport where
I couldn't have felt more alone despite being bumped
and shuffled by the pressing crowd following the arrow
out or back standing still at one point I realized till
knocked rudely to my senses and I moved again
with purpose shouldering my bag for every member of
my sex the swelling surge again of being who else
dared do what I was doing? the answer unfortunately
coming all too quickly those looking for jihad women
anxious to notch themselves to the cogs of the ideal

Islamic state and me was I so different in my
submission to Ukraine? no it was not submission I
asserted boldly if comically lifting chin and pressing on into
a hail of gunfire and exploding shells ducking then
in the mix to dart low through the colored mess of
sonic and spatial indifference so low my nose was
scraping the dirt rushing forward breathing in and out the
choking guilt of personal and feminist failure

XXVII

The beard was certainly familiar but the face above it
meant nothing to me my fingers laced through the strands
of that hair that twirled black and gray longly from his
chin some time ago as in a dream or in wisps of smoke lying
with him that beard anyway in the dark the black beard
the only thing of light in the room lying with him
muttering conclusions or promises of how the world
should be or is or was when we were younger and would
be again lying with him seeming to make it possible the
world and I rebooted to the start of civilization and we

rushed out then headlong into that fresh orange world dashing with thick black lines trailing after evidencing our speed to where? with that beard flowing back too over shoulder run! I heard him slice in a whisper that cut through the exploding night like a missile and then I lost him and was alone huddled somewhere in a corner with knees bent up fingers still twitching as if tangling beard

XXVIII

Ed had had enough by that time the signs clear enough then that I intended to go away and there was little which is to say nothing that Ed could do about it was only a matter now of retreat and how best to pull that off although when honest with himself he knew he much preferred to simply dash off and dispense with all the worry over production of presenting himself in such a way as to make his exodus a performance of great beguiling destruction a slipping away into the waiting jaws of oblivion its stale breath colored to swallow one in the warm human swamp dump the indulgent comfort of nostalgic misery the reality being that most likely no one was even prepared to watch him go no matter how he went or even notice at the end of it that he was gone there'd be no ransom for his safe return no heartfelt or perfunctory plea for his recapture his release back into the celebrated arms of quotidian obsolescence

So he fell off and rebounded time and again leaving no mark nor making any statement littering the pathways to escape with a constant ebb and flow of effectiveness and its counter going yet remaining set off from the daily décor by the thinnest of lines inked to destroy nothing to accomplish nothing sitting and waiting and expiring blinking off and on like an unnoticed Christmas light a beacon in a sea of them one star in the sky twinkling dimly with the rest a patchwork of blunted passions of weak desires bludgeoned into the boring ache of forgetfulness into dull stretching extension he stood up from this once and moved on swiftly but only came to sit down again

Where were you born? they asked him but he couldn't readily supply an answer whom have you involved yourself with? the meaning of which didn't even register what will be your salvation? nothing that he could think of but maybe he hadn't thought enough about it or at all but it seemed now that they wouldn't let him be free of the question salvation not a matter of take it or leave it but of where and when accepted or enforced pick your poison

When he awoke within it or to it although to be sure he couldn't say exactly what it was he found himself filled with a feeling of exalted relief a sensation akin to leaving the office for a long weekend the difference here being that there didn't appear to be an end to this weekend on the horizon it was a smoothly paved road leading out through rows of manicured trees leaves drifting down in quiet orchestrated perfection happily leading nowhere but never dipping into night never scrubbing the stomach raw pulsing with the solar drive of early sunny afternoon going but remaining the path never altered by the torture of

timekeeping or moving
    Conversion felt inevitable
    He would go

XXIX

It had begun and I was in deep somehow I woke in that dark basement I say basement but really I have no idea where the room was in relation to the earth a man seated propped in the corner his pants down at his ankles yoking one leg to the other in a bundling of thick camouflaged cotton directly above still laced military boots his genitals replaced with a hard masking of dried blood frayed wires or veins sprouting from the mess to drape over splayed lifeless thighs

I left him there and went out fueled by a

purpose I couldn't articulate to reunite the state to be sure but without a firm understanding of what such a unification might look like nor what degree of destruction might be necessary to abort the unhealthy elements to sift the cancerous ignorance and its progenitors out from green growth to cultivate the spread of sustainable democratic rule predicated on informed consent and bolstered by a citizenry eager to contain itself and its ambitions which is to say to reject growth in the physical realm wrest expansive control from the corporate slime oozing its filth yet was that the plan here? was it really what the people and by extension I myself wanted what we were fighting for? I toted my elephant gun with a righteous indignation that I couldn't be sure wouldn't warp the barrel back my way and in a desperate shot obliterate the whole hazy system of eyes that might already be blind

But the alternative it seemed was simply to lie down and be run over be trampled by the roiling boots of blitzing tyranny

XXX

I hadn't seen Ed for ages by that point or so it seemed the travel no doubt and the commotion warping time to a great extent which nevertheless didn't make the time gap any shorter or less real nor had I received any word from him or tried in any way to reach him a quarantine from one another that he likewise observed of his own volition we had not previously planned to stay out of touch although in doing so I at least felt like I was adhering to an agreed upon course that was no less in force simply by not having been discussed the unspoken agreement in fact pointing at least in my mind to a bond whose strength had not made itself evident during the time we were actually together but now reared its ugly head if I may be permitted to use such a tired cliché even when it's not particularly true neither Ed nor the relationship being in fact ugly drawing me back toward him if only in weak emotional moments of which thankfully there were few given all the pressing and present distractions exploding all around me physical exertion and peril driving every thought not connected to the moment to my survival the survival of others and to self-determination out of my mind to be considered if reformed later or not one kept a steel clean mind here shimmering and invigoratingly cold focused on implementing the solution which perhaps was never at any given moment illuminated with a defining clarity but hopscotched its way to an end which indeed was well known articulated and broadcast for all in the world to understand if not follow the dismantling of this separatist secessionist movement now even voted upon in an election widely condemned for its illegality and insistence for not only continuing but broadening strikes against the established democracy renewing strikes against Mariupol Dubalsiva and the airport in Donetsk with word coming down that Sunday night as I recall coming down a way to describe the nebulous nature of such news and its pathways though to be sure we a group of 4 or 5 or perhaps 10 or 12 or 50 or 2 of us I was not alone certainly found ourselves in a small poorly lit room huddled you might say discussing passionately the arrival of this news bequeathed from the ether that the separatists would be gathering in a theater in Donetsk to inaugurate install anoint what have you the new leader of their secessionist game and we were to decide what we might if anything do about it whether through word or through force though it was vibrantly clear from the start from the mood in the room that the word would never carry the day a sweat bubbling for action humidified ceiling walls and all cubic space caught within draining foreheads of reason perhaps but inflaming murderous passions to be sure so that a plan was quickly if in hindsight too quickly formed and we had paired off suited up and headed out in ridiculous regrettable again as seen from a future perspective comic book fashion the world an automatic warzone governed by the muscled flight of too ready brawn and fingers itching to trigger meaning through murder not exactly mindless but miscellaneous nonetheless a target picked as much for its not you see for his or her but its power of the hour as perceived by unknown unknowable people or powers more accurately or so it seemed the true face of victim nor perpetrator ever clearly seen but projected in hi-def in the mind's eye relieving any doubt as to the necessity of the project the synaptic assurance firing the bullet as surely as the finger the victim dead first and in a manner primarily in the warthreaded webbing of the mind where it might remain dead or be reborn later according to flashing cerebral dictates and the ever extending pattern of cognition lacing waves of thought experience and ambition into infinite sheets of crosshairing nubs the one that night centering collectively it might be said on one Alexander Zakharchenko with the aim of preventing him from ascending to the exalted position of head to the separatist body politic and thus our sworn enemy or so it seemed at the time although cleaner smoke swabbed heads would've seen the futility the nonconsequentialism in it from the start that not only would our small band of patriotic mercenaries prove incapable of pulling off this little stunt so poor were our powers of forethought that we never envisioned the heavily armed guard detail we would meet but even if we had been capable of executing that assassination it would have amounted to nothing greater than felling a weed in a field where thousands more might spring up and in fact be compelled to do so by the sudden hewing of their master from his roots if the biology of the metaphor carries we surmounted hills overlooking the site and slithered down on our bellies becoming then aware of the troops massed about the theater as we emerged from the shadows woefully unprepared to exercise the plans drawn out or perhaps only imagined in the heated confines of our little room I recall slinging rifle round from my back and propping myself low on elbows and waiting freezing in the moment and unable to go on the streetlamps shed a broad and flatly cruel penetrating light that seared in its coldness threatening in every descending lumen to betray the positions we had crept into at the base of the hill everything turned to stone sticking us like statues perhaps mistaken by our opponents for street art constructed or at least placed there by the democratic regime they now railed against and perhaps

it was nothing more than disgust and the itch for a bit of
fun that caused them suddenly to spray our positions
with gunfire

XXXI

While dark outside a bright sun-like exuberance cut
through the window sparking a room white and waiting
to be fulfilled his grandmother came over and sat next to
him on the sofa the davenport maybe carrying something
like a platter of cookies the platter also white and fluted
mirroring to a certain extent the plentiful soft pleats in
his grandmother's cheeks the daylight full and hot as the
clock pushed on into night I've been feeling rather
out of sorts Ed admitted to his grandmother as she
poured the tea nodding warmly the brown stream filling

into the waiting complacent china as the too pleasant filling of wasted time causing him to sigh in spite of himself whatever that might mean you'll figure it out his grandmother was saying which he knew to be only empty grandmotherly kindness but added a certain warmth to the room nonetheless humming beneath the sharp ascending steam

Lifting his cup to lips Ed sipped the sweet hot tea savoring its milkiness in swallow hoping the warmth of the liquid might spread and overtake his body his head rub his eyes into sleep but the tea only seemed to make him more alert more on edge and he set the cup down abruptly

Outside a man with a flashlight was hunting for something at the edge of the yard the full blackness of the night now causing the man's form to illuminate only in what light might reflect back from the beam of his tool and then only in an illumination of the darkest gray the slightest protuberance punched from the night the tight yellow circle of light before him and its attendant beam dancing in a rhythmic scribble both exhilarating and hypnotizing that brought Ed out to the yard with him searching mining the grass for examples of wet swollen life lost betwixt the blades glandular creatures inching about the lawn like amputated thumbs

His grandmother began to cough which Ed couldn't help but find annoying who's that man out there? he asked he didn't want to have to deal with one of his grandmother's coughing fits what man? which just as easily could have been what mack? the final word loosed from ravaged lungs that continued backfiring then for some time next it would be a trip to urgent care and an afternoon lost but no it was already night and there was a man in the garden did his grandmother have a garden? sputtering his flashlight to the rhythm of his grandmother's coughing a percussion and light show that made him for a time forget where he was till at some point his grandmother asked again what man? clearly this time maybe it's not a man Ed told her just as the flashlight went out I'm not sure his grandmother hummed something and nodded an understanding lifting her tea cup returning the room to night

XXXII

It started after the assassination attempt the returning itch to feed my days with heroin honestly I had seldom thought about heroin during the previous 12 months or more maybe it had been all the distractions but in truth as far as I can recollect there hadn't been any more distractions during the previous year than usual and it was distractions that finally brought the insistent fingers back picking at me trying to gain entrance not leaving me alone promising they'd settle down if I just gave them what they wanted the argument persuasive after all after all the months of being silent of being nonexistent coming back scratching up all those old feelings that I had happily relinquished or so I'd thought like a switch flicked and I was on again the difference being that I did have some defenses in place I was cognizant of addiction and my addiction more personally and had acquired ways of thinking about it and about dealing with temptation if that's even the right word to use to describe the pull of junk so it was not like a wave rushing in overwhelming me even as the deep blood tingling began to bubble up I was surprised nothing more or perhaps also a bit annoyed and then slowly fearful which begins the dangerous and exponentially more fearful slip wherein all your well-forged and well-planted brakes break away or more accurately dissolve or evaporate leaving not the slightest evidence save your faint and no doubt even at that inaccurate memories that they ever existed sliding the G-force of temptation or inevitability increasing as you go down so that it becomes next to impossible to imagine yourself operating without the slick heroin comfort the drive especially in moments of war which were new to me then and I awoke suddenly realizing that I was in wholly new unfamiliar territory with nary a friend nor even an acquaintance not struck in the previous weeks around about me and I realized suddenly that I was now dealing quite literally with fire gunfire and what else? death an all too real reality what else can one do?

XXXIII

We are increasingly nowhere he said pressing himself betwixt the tank and brick wall and continuing sideways along the passage without losing as much as a step of speed so it was hard for me to keep up and indeed I lost the next bundling of words cast from his mouth into the battered bricks hastening then to close the distance between us as he was saying cut their breasts clean off them the bodies burned to charred blackness it's not human the things they do I nodded eagerly in agreement although he was turned away from me looking forward so there was in effect no purpose to my nodding we cleared the wall then and the tank which in retrospect must have been several tanks lined end to end and were struck suddenly by an unfriendly blast of wind like a smack to the face from a frozen hand and again more of the commander's words were lost to the icy swirling environs

He walked briskly across the yard his stride the product of a strong well-oiled machinery of legs that quickened also my heart or cooch to be less romantic and more accurate seemingly without purpose at first his destination unknown to me till he strode up to and stopped in front of a bulky man who wore a heavy clod of dark, mud-colored hair plastered atop his bulbous 40-something head the two exchanged several urgent sentences directives and confirmations I heard clearly at the time but the content of which escapes me now and we moved on then I following without knowing if my pursuit was still desired the uneasiness rising suddenly within me or had I ever been meant to follow him?

We went inside a stale poorly heated place filled

with desks and tables and chairs hastily placed across the large open room to form a makeshift office it hummed like a small machine shop the voices coiled into a hearty rumble that gave the confidence of competent orchestrated action the commander snaked between the people and furniture maneuvering like a practiced athlete the obstacles that hung me up again and again till I feared I would be trapped finally corralled by some improbable shifting of hundred-pound desks monstrous stacks of paper and bodies planted in their chairs sealing me in without notice and my voice too thin or humble to carry my protestations to effect I brushed a piling of papers with my knees or shins sending them in a fearful slide floorward but kept on walking refusing to look back or to the side and face any awoken glares keeping my eyes pinned to the commander's broad wool shoulders that seemed always to be pulling farther away from me

When I caught up to him he was stationed in front of a drab metal desk speaking to an equally drab woman sitting behind it her face a dusty shade of vanilla with its particulars arranged in such a manner as to give the appearance she was being seen in a mirror a once familiar face rendered joltingly backwards although of course I had never seen her before that moment yes they were indeed very polite the commander asked her ushered me to my destination with their rifles he frowned have you seen the little green men? she said I was doing nothing more than walking the streets he put to her then minding my own business running errands you know? the woman shook her head and what were you up to? the commander unbuttoned his coat you have no idea he inquired of her I'm sure they understood perfectly she said sucking in her lips

A portly sergeant materialized beside her standing out of breath holding a tower of papers that wavered precariously perched on forearms extended straight out from his ample belly his badly scuffed and beaten uniform which once must have been quite the spectacle a dazzling canary-colored number sufficiently roughed up now to supply the requisite friction to keep the papers from spilling over onto desk and floor

We need to start all over the commander said casting a disturbed more annoyance than concern eye at the sergeant's pile of papers which might become a huge mess at any moment his voice and manner bespeaking bold new action but neither he nor the woman nor the sergeant moved from their spots or gave any indication that they intended to act in any way on the commander's directive their statuary stances broken only by a sudden waft of cabbage scent to wrinkle noses everything is rotten the commander mumbling but it will come back

Looking then upon the woman behind the desk I had to blink and recalibrate my eyes assuring the weary orbs that this was in fact the same woman as before such had been her transformation from seconds earlier a true beauty now with years removed and features realigned luxurious hair piled and falling the commander smiled upon her it's crazy to imagine why anyone would need to look beyond earth to find beauty he said or maybe just his look and smile said this the sergeant meanwhile had flushed considerably his exposed skin so inflamed as to lend a reddish tint even to his tarnished yellow suit head cocked oddly directing gaze down toward the світська дама bubbles percolating carelessly from his lips those of the commander parting to speak though he was suddenly far away when he spoke the following or so I imagined him or imagine him now she will be the salvation of us all he purred his voice escaping into a tunnel of sorts before wholly dissipating

I thought then of Ed for some reason and I grew very cold

She's growing a voice very much like the commander's said from some locale far afield and indeed the woman behind the desk did seem to be expanding inflating although time proved that she was instead lifting rising up from her seat like a saint drifting lazily skyward legs crossed like the Buddha a sublime trace of a smile brightening her lips slowly up hovering awhile till then rising quietly more and passing through the roof or perhaps she slipped into another dimension then and there without rising any further her youthful puff received as a Ukrainian Assumption a deliverance to or from something that none of us in the room surely understood though the sergeant's papers finally did spill in the draft of this miracle and his belly wretched and shrunk something horrible so that I couldn't bear to look at him any longer and in fact felt myself stricken by a commanding distaste for all things male for the brutish thrust of penile action and inaction we should all be very concerned the commander said then sternly clamping his jaw shut turning and marching from the room

XXXIV

Soon after our second shot we got down to discussing terrestrial matters even as our heads swam liquid ease waving at passing galaxies I fear the commander will not be back he said sipping now hot spiced tea I nodded to convey complete stern agreement although in truth I was far from certain about anything and knew nothing about the commander's whereabouts or intentions did you hear what the Chechen stooge Kadyrov said about the Islamic attack in Grozny? he asked of course I hadn't I no longer seemed to hear anything he flew home whipped up a special operation and killed the devils here he shook his head held some meetings and still made it back to Moscow to hear dear leader Putin speak grinning dirty what a fuckin badass Kadyrov is no? no I agreed for I was truly disgusted by the flippant warmongering attitude but not just Kadyrov's but everyone's everywhere back in the US the streets were filling well at least in certain sections of certain streets in certain sections of certain cities with people protesting police brutality white against black gunning down unarmed black men and children with impunity Michael Brown Eric Garner Tamir Rice and on and on and on the Justice Department leveling judgment against Cleveland's police department for excessive use of force inadequate and insufficient training and accountability and on and on and on and I wondered then heartsick how Ed as a black man was faring that night

XXXV

Somewhere on a hidden radio on a hidden shelf somewhere Sinatra's Before the Music Ends was playing with all its ridiculous bombast syrupy strains of sentimentality trying to cement in etched record grooves the legacy of one who needed no such treatment who's stature had already been sealed by the great records not about himself the record droned painfully on as Francis visited Hoboken schoolyards and pool halls then took a last stab at Vegas with Dino and Sarge all so pathetic and inadequate to express what it is to remember or regret or dream or be touched by the passage of time and yet is not that clichéd overreach the standard of our lives? is it not what we all rely on when it comes down to it? is it not what drives us off to war and into beds and office buildings with inadequate unsatisfying sparring partners hoping to capture the impossible coupling the explosive tangling incarnate the renewal that ultimately repudiates itself yet without the rebuke stinging us straight smart returning always to whatever it was to again not capture what is impossible to capture and sing about it to the mirror?

Ed was perhaps wandering his hometown city streets much like the aged Francis or so I imagined which was silly of course the age difference being quite severe and I can't say what compelled me to think of him in that manner though in truth he always had something of the wanderer about him and the aged and the worn all the time I knew him wandering like all wanderers without destination but also without much if any desire to stumble onto a destination which I think he would find not only restrictive but defining in such a way as to be restrictive as all definitions are but I couldn't place him at all in these imagined wanderings he didn't visit any of the places that we went together but rather trudged through gray watercolor landscapes that grew darker as he passed bleeding into a deep ink blackness that washed away his features till finally I lost sight of him

We were now pushing those who might be allies in the East further east toward Putin some felt particularly by our refusal meaning Kiev's refusal to cut ties with the neo-Nazi Azov battalion that continued to fight in Eastern Ukraine and through sanctions against the East freezing government pensions and cutting off funding for schools and hospitals actions it was argued that hurt the people not the rebels and provided Putin with ready-made propaganda it made me sick I was through I felt without knowing entirely what I was through with or not willing to accept that my throughness applied nearly to everything in the US the Senate had finally released findings of secret CIA torture post-9/11 and while there was certainly widespread outrage over the report's findings many others came forward to vehemently defend the use of torture and insist upon its efficacy and therefore its righteousness I was sick of it all nothing seemed worth fighting for in this crazy despicable world in which tangled in every movement or desire were the threads of rabid boastful inhumanity cast as the pure strands of unsentimental understanding I was sick and yet relieved at least for a time that my sickness did not drive me toward the nonrelief relief through drugs but even that victory didn't satisfy for more than a few seconds and even quickly turned into defeat I no longer cared enough even to try and find a way to relieve the pain the emptiness of uncaring or rather I realized there was no relief no relief from anything just different modes of misery my coming here my so-called freedom fighting was just more shifting futility like Sinéad O'Connor's joining of the Sinn Féin party and calling on all its leaders to step down in favor of younger ones just a recycling of well-meaning futile action all leading to exhaustion and misery ridiculous

XXXVI

Not long after that I was heading back home although truth be told I no longer thought or felt more accurately of it as home it was simply a place to return to a chance to reset and as I collapsed into my seat on the airplane a bit lightheaded from being whisked through the security lines I exhaled months' worth of exhaustion which up to that point I hadn't realized I'd been holding onto the great hassle of living and of always trying to accomplish something or at least always feeling the need the pressure to accomplish something to do great things which of course is what gives us humans value a measure a stacking up which too often also results in a stacking up of bodies slain I was sick of it but sick too of its continuing inevitability which is to say that I knew once I got over this particularly strong bout of sickness that I would once again cheer up and become inspired as they say and zip off to do great wondrous things to make my mark I nearly hurled just thinking about it with the zing of a personal final solution electrifying my mind then once the acid in my gut had dissipated sparking the idea suddenly of suicide which liquefied my body into the warm comfort of giving up a terror of course resignation the gravest sin so to distract myself from it I accessed my email on my phone scrolling through weeks' perhaps months' worth of messages most of which were completely unfamiliar to me though I had obviously already read them once which is to say I had already clicked on them once without however having paid much if any attention to them so that buried within the mess which to be sure was with the very rare exception not at all worth reading I came across a message from Ed which I was likewise ignorant of a fact which caused me a considerable amount of consternation of disappointment in myself for my lack of caring or maybe more accurately disappointment in myself for not caring that I didn't care I opened the message whose subject was I'll Be Around… and read the curt instruction within Don't try to find me when you get back, I won't be around I laughed audibly perhaps or maybe not the note striking me as wholly pathetic a put-on something that meant to say exactly the opposite of what on its face it was pretending to say the subject line to my thinking confirming this notion the reference obviously to the old song I'll be around no matter how you treat me now he'd be around all right and his little passive-aggressive denial of such had the immediate effect of causing me never to want to see him again which I was happy to know wasn't at all the effect he had intended

But was it wise or right? just? just to let him be?

XXXVII

In those days the ruble was sinking or it had already sunk
Russian bank officials eager to prevent inflation raised the
interest rate from 10.5% to 17% the biggest hike since the
country's default in 1998 served them right in a sense but
who was it really hurting? Putin wasn't missing any
meals that's for sure nor were any of the rest of the
oligarchs but as always it was the people who were
suffering from the US-led Western sanctions and when I
returned home barely had I settled in or so it seems now
recalling than I was on the rapid heading off downtown to

the library to immerse myself in economic texts
volumes upon volumes I pored through sticking mostly
to the established and not so established radicals Keynes Marx
Daly I see myself sitting at the library's heavy wooden desks
day after day for several weeks on end although likely it was no
more than a week altogether economic tomes stacked on either
side of the one currently open in front of me the desk's
green shaded lamp on as the winter afternoon grew dark
outside this is what I remember along with a vague but
very satisfying taste of papery intelligence that I gulped with
gluttonous unconcern but of the works themselves of the
theories and the recommended actions I remember almost
nothing

XXXVIII

Suddenly it dawned on me if anyone was to look for and find Ed it would have to be me looking back on this assessment I have to admit that it lacks quite a bit in terms of intellectual vigor and credibility there was really no reason why I should be the one to look for Ed in fact there were probably plenty of other people far more qualified than me although I would not be able to provide you with any names or even personality traits skills or education but at the time suddenly as I have said I was convinced that it was me or no one and so that's why I began

At first I did very little often sitting still in my apartment or in the café that Ed and I used to frequent allowing inspiration to wash over me which is to say doing nothing since inspiration never washed over me but at best spit drops of intimation or knowing that awoke me with their cold prick of wetness on the forehead the flash of a picture a face a place a scent or sound that seemed tangentially related to Ed but then just as quickly evaporated into apartment or café air leaving nothing more than the tracing of a trace of understanding and connection which dredged deeper troughs of emptiness in my already vacant brain nothing was getting started and after a while that became intolerantly unpleasant so I got up finally from my sitting and went out to the street and started walking stumbling finally upon a rally for Michael Brown and Tamir Rice although stumbling of course couldn't be accurate neither in a literal nor figurative sense for I was not physically impaired nor it seems to me now could I have happened upon such a protest accidentally it's possible of course but seems so unlikely as to be safely ruled an impossibility which means I must have known about the protest and set out that day either consciously or unconsciously to find it and take part lacing in with those who had traveled from Ferguson to participate which is to say that I too was something of a foreigner among the protesters from my own town and quite consciously so on that occasion the gut stab of social shirking of bitching but not doing

I lay then on the pavement and spread my arms wide

Dying

Later and whether it was later that day as I remember or the next day or the next I can't faithfully say I wandered into the Ukrainian Museum-Archives on Kenilworth not to imply that there's any other such Ukrainian establishment in town which I had certainly known about for ages but had never managed to find my way into with the long-unfulfilled objective of investigating the blasphemy charges leveled against the venerated Ukrainian poet and painter Taras Shevchenko during an 1859 and final trip to his homeland which to be truthful was mostly a ruse my investigative urge that is to gain purposeful entry to the UMA and see what it was all about although I was in fact curious to learn which of Shevchenko's actions or thoughts had been deemed blasphemous and also the character blasphemy charges took more generally at the time I entered to warm reception which reminds me now that my visit could not have occurred so soon after my participation in the protest the visit that I am recalling here that is since I was greeted on that occasion by the archive's resident scholar who had already prepared some materials for my visit so this must have been later after I had already dropped in once before and learned that the archives were only available by appointment but on that occasion the scholar settled me down in a room upstairs with a Shevchenko biography and a couple volumes of his artwork along with helpful guidance from the scholar himself and I was free to explore the matter in winter quiet early afternoon

Shevchenko stood with Volsky as the latter bent eye to surveyor's glass measuring the lot for a small cottage Shevchenko was thinking of building on the property that he was thinking of buying when cross the field clomped Kozlovsky a cousin of Volsky's decked out in his Sunday best and nice threads! quipped Shevchenko employing perhaps some more era-appropriate dig to which Kozlovsky nevertheless took universal umbrage and the poet quickly leveled an apology accompanied possibly by a friendly clap on the shoulder and the trio went off after the surveying was finished to a local haunt for dinner and all was forgiven until at least Kozlovsky twixt pork chop and claret or vodka or such trumpeted a theological discussion which was in no manner to Shevchenko's liking so out he spurted Shevchenko that is that theology without a living god cannot create even one living leaf which effectively silenced matters for a time during which Shevchenko and his companions fell back to eating and to drinking of course but Kozlovsky yet was not to be denied completely and soon enough started in again with his theological line of chat asking Shevchenko what he thought about the Virgin mother to which Shevchenko replied that she should indeed be honored for giving birth to Christ for failing that she'd have been just an ordinary woman well that was simply too much for poor Kozlovsky to swallow and he notified apparently the appropriate authorities if in fact he was not himself such an official specifically tasked with inciting Shevchenko to such damning talk the result whatever the case being that Shevchenko was arrested a week later while crossing over the Dnieper and charged with blasphemy a matter that came to be handled by Prince Vasilchikov the governor general who judged the thing basically a misunderstanding but advised which is to say ordered Shevchenko to leave Ukraine nonetheless which he did never to return his plans to settle and maybe marry in his native land scuttled by mixing and drinking with strangers and as typical for the poet in such situations blabbing too much

Out once again in the cold I stood dumb for a measure or two till my senses recalibrated from inside and overly warm to outside and shockingly cold and then I turned and walked east to the corner and then made a left going north up West 11th a block to reach Loop the café and record store which I entered it seems quite hastily fairly charging up the steps and forcefully swinging open the door to present myself heart racing to the curious if not suspicious baristas I nodded as friendly as I might though I recall the action being as rushed and as awkward as desperate as my entrance had been and walked hopefully with some semblance of calm to the stairs and went up to where the records were on the second floor and only when I was properly stationed in front of the bin of jazz records that is only after I had installed myself there giving myself discernible purpose was I able to release my breath which I seemed to have been holding since stepping onto the sidewalk outside the UMA flipping through LPs that to the touch to the sight seemed at once odd and familiar Ed was more the jazz listener whereas I typically poked around the edges and never got excited about the discovery of unknown combos or long-sought-after releases I of course had no long-sought-after releases but merely enjoyed the good tune or two if I was in the mood yet there I was flipping through the records the credible hipster vinyl junkie and even found myself not only engaged in the process but sparked occasionally by a familiar name or particularly attractive cover

That day I bought a copy of Sun Ra's Other Planes of There with the spiral line drawing on the cover rendered by Ra himself a purchase that certainly would have pleased Ed took it home played it and discovered that I liked the record very much

ABOUT THE AUTHOR

MATT MARSHALL is the author of the novel, *The Starlight Line*. He contributes regularly to the online jazz publication *All About Jazz*. His work has also appeared in *Jazz Inside Magazine*, *Cleveland Scene*, *Cleveland Free Times*, *Free Inquiry* and various print and online literary journals. He lives in Cleveland Heights, Ohio.

mattmarshallwriter.com